Magic
Animal Friends

For Maggie Rose

Special thanks to Valerie Wilding

No part of this publication may be reproduced, stored in a retrieval system, or transmitted in any form or by any means, electronic, mechanical, photocopying, recording, or otherwise, without written permission of the publisher. For information regarding permission, write to Working Partners Limited, 9 Kingsway, 4th Floor, London WC2B 6XF, United Kingdom.

ISBN 978-0-545-94076-4

Printed in the U.S.A.   40
First printing 2016

Olivia Nibblesqueak's Messy Mischief

Daisy Meadows

Scholastic Inc.

Can you keep a secret? I thought you could!

Then I'll tell you about an enchanted wood.

It lies through the door in the old oak tree,

Let's go there now—just follow me!

We'll find adventure that never ends,

And meet the Magic Animal Friends!

Love,
Goldie the Cat

Contents

CHAPTER ONE

A Special Day

"I think these are ready," said Jess Forester, sniffing the freshly baked animal treats that were cooling on the table.

"Great!" said her best friend, Lily Hart. "Now we can go and help with the feeding time!"

The girls packed up the treats and left

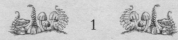

Lily's house, heading for the barn at the bottom of her yard. But this was no ordinary barn, it was the Helping Paw Wildlife Hospital, which was run by Lily's parents! Lily and Jess both adored animals and loved helping to care for them whenever they could. Luckily Jess only lived across the street from her best friend.

It was a bright autumn day and warm sunshine was glinting on the red and orange leaves in the trees. Lily's mom was putting fresh hay into the rabbit and guinea pig runs.

Lily held the treats. "Look, Mom! Dad

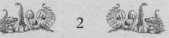

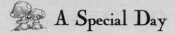

helped us make these treats from oats, grated carrots, and ripe bananas."

Mrs. Hart peered at them. "Mmm, they look delicious!" she said, grinning.

"They're not for people, they're for the animals!" Jess laughed. She knew Lily's mom was teasing.

While Mrs. Hart went back into the hospital for more food, the girls put a handful of treats in the rabbit run. The bunnies' noses went *woffle woffle* as they sniffed the

air, their whiskers

quivering, then

nibbled the

treats.

"Aren't they

sweet?" said Lily. "They

remind me of the animals enjoying

yummy food at the Toadstool Café."

The girls grinned at each other. The

Toadstool Café was in Friendship Forest,

a magical world where animals lived in

beautiful little cottages and dens. But the

most amazing thing about Friendship

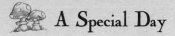

Forest was that all the creatures there could talk!

"I wonder when we'll see Goldie again," said Jess, thinking about the beautiful cat that took them to the forest. "It's so much fun talking to the animals."

"And sharing adventures with them!" added Lily.

They heard a soft mew. From behind a hutch a sweet golden face appeared, with eyes as green as new grass.

"Goldie!" the girls cried in delight. The cat bounded over and rubbed against their legs, purring. Then she turned toward Brightley Stream, which ran at the end of the Harts' yard, and mewed again.

"She wants us to follow her," cried Jess, her eyes shining. "We're going back to Friendship Forest!"

Filled with excitement, the girls raced after Goldie, their feet rustling the leaves that lay all around. They went over the stepping stones that crossed the stream and into Brightley Meadow. Ahead of them was a huge, dead oak tree.

Right before their eyes, the branches burst into new life. Scarlet berries

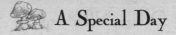

hung from every bough and bluebirds
swooped between the branches, singing
a joyful song.

Goldie mewed and put a paw up to
touch the tree, and some letters appeared,
carved into the tree's bark.

The girls clasped hands and read the words aloud. "Friendship Forest!"

A door with a leaf-shaped handle appeared in the trunk. When Jess opened it, shimmering golden light shone from inside. Goldie ran through the doorway.

Jess grinned at Lily. "I wonder what adventure we'll have this time?"

The girls' hearts raced as they followed Goldie into the light, and their bodies tingled all over as they shrank, just a little.

As the glow faded, Jess and Lily found themselves in a clearing in Friendship

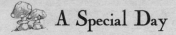

Forest. The air was warm and filled with the scent of cotton-candy flowers.

"Welcome back," said Goldie's soft voice.

The girls turned. The cat, now wearing a golden scarf, stood upright, as tall as their shoulders. She ran to hug them. "I've got a surprise for you!" she said.

Wondering what it could be, the girls followed Goldie. Their friend's tail was twitching with excitement as they passed little cottages nestled between tree roots and perched on branches. But none of their animal friends were waving from the windows like they usually did.

"Friendship Forest seems really quiet today, Goldie," said Jess. "Is there something happening?"

The cat smiled. "You'll see," she said.

As they reached a small clearing, a delicious aroma wafted toward them. Lots of different animals were crowded outside a pretty little pink cottage. Now the girls knew why they hadn't seen any of their friends—everybody was here!

"Look at all the cakes and buns!" said Jess. "That's what the yummy smell is—baking!"

Goldie smiled again. "See the sign above the door?"

"*The Nibblesqueak Bakery,*" Lily read.

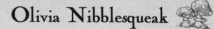

"It's the grand opening today," said Goldie, "and the Nibblesqueak family are having a cake-decorating contest. Everyone's invited." Her green eyes shone. "Come on—let's help them celebrate!"

CHAPTER TWO

Splat!

A family of golden-brown hamsters was handing out cakes to the other animals, who were sitting at the tables outside the bakery. They waved and came over to greet the girls.

"Lily and Jess, meet Mr. and Mrs. Nibblesqueak," Goldie said, "and their

children, Penny, Jenny, and Olivia." Each
little hamster wore a garland of flowers

on her head. Olivia's
was made of roses,
and, as the girls
bent down to say
hello, she slipped
her tiny paw into
Jess's hand.

"It's really nice to meet you," the little
hamster said in a sweet voice.

More of the girls' friends crowded
around. "Hello!" cried Molly Twinkletail,
the tiny mouse.

 14

"Hello, Jess and Lily!" Bella Tabbypaw, a striped silver cat with a pink backpack, called out.

"Hooray, you're back!" said Emily Prickleback the hedgehog.

"It's lovely to see you all!" Lily replied, hugging them. The girls had helped Molly, Bella, and Emily when they'd been in trouble, and they had been good friends ever since.

Emily took Jess and Lily to watch the young animals decorating cakes at a long table. They were squeezing colored icing from little bags with nozzles on them.

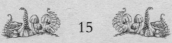

"I love those swirly patterns you're making," said Lily.

"And the tiny flowers," added Jess.

"Thank you, thank you!" all the little animals squeaked.

Lily looked at the cottage. "Isn't it pretty, Jess?" she said.

The bakery roof was thatched with reeds. The ground floor was a shop, and the girls kneeled down to peer through the tiny windows. Dozens of tiny cakes were laid out on a counter, all decorated with pretty icing. "It's so sweet," said Jess. "And everything looks yummy!"

 16

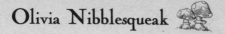

As Lily was looking through the
upstairs windows, where there were little
beds with frilly covers, she felt someone
tapping her foot. She looked down and
saw Olivia carrying a large bowl
and smiling happily.

"Do you want to try some icing?"
asked the hamster, showing them
the creamy white mixture. "Only we
Nibblesqueaks know the secret of making
our famous Nectar Icing. It's delicious!
Come and see!"

She took the girls to a table and picked
up a bag with a nozzle. "Mr. Cleverfeather

the owl invented this," she said. "It's an Eezy-Skweezy Icing Bag."

Olivia twiddled a dial beside the nozzle. "You turn this for different colors," she explained, and squeezed rose-pink icing onto a cake.

A little vole wearing blue sneakers came over. "Olivia, I ran out again," he said, sheepishly.

The hamster smiled. "Percy Littlepaw!" she said. "That was your third bag! Never mind, you can share mine." She turned to the girls and whispered, "Percy's my best friend. He loves icing so much, I think he must be eating it all!"

Percy started scampering off with the icing, then gave a shout. "Look out!"

Splat!

The new sign above the door was smeared with splattered cake!

"Who did that?" wondered Olivia, turning around.

"Heeheehee!"

Jess looked around, but couldn't see where the giggling came from, then . . .

Splat!

"Hey!" cried Percy as a cake hit him right in the face.

Percy wiped pink icing from his cheek and giggled as he licked his paw clean. But then the animals shrieked and scattered as more cakes zoomed over. *Splat, splat, splat!*

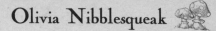

The flying cakes covered everything with bits of sponge and icing.

Jess and Lily glanced at each other in amazement. Someone was throwing cakes! But who?

CHAPTER THREE

Creatures from the Witchy Waste

Olivia and Lily helped Percy tidy up, while Jess searched nearby bushes, looking for whoever was throwing the cakes. But she couldn't see anyone.

"Who spoiled our competition?" wailed Penny Nibblesqueak.

"And ruined our cakes!" said her sister Jenny, sadly.

Jess turned anxiously to Goldie and Lily. "Do you think Grizelda is behind this?" she whispered.

Grizelda was a witch who wanted Friendship Forest for herself. She kept looking for ways to force all the animals to leave. First, she'd used her smelly helpers, the Boggits, to try to drive the animals out. When that had failed, she'd kidnapped four baby dragons and made them help her instead. But so far, Lily, Jess, and Goldie had always managed to defeat her.

"It could be Grizelda," Goldie said, looking anxious. "Maybe she has a nasty new plan?"

Lily hugged her. "If she does, we'll stop her somehow," she said. "Won't we, Jess?"

Jess nodded. "We'll do anything to protect Friendship Forest!" Then she gave a cry. "There, under that table! I saw a paw! Look, there it is again!"

A dirty paw appeared and threw a bowl of yellow icing.

Crash!

The bowl broke, splattering blobs of icing all over the grass.

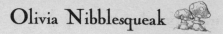

"It could be another dragon!" cried Mrs. Nibblesqueak. "Quick, little ones, get into the bakery!"

The animals ran for cover, but Lily, Jess, and Goldie darted over to the table and peered underneath. Four grubby looking creatures with bold expressions stared back at them. There was a black

bat with stained wings and a scruffy tie around his neck, and a warty green toad, covered in slime. Next to them were a crow with messy, smelly feathers and a rat with dirty, clumped fur. And their paws were all covered in cake!

"Stop that!" cried Lily. "You're making an awful mess."

The filthy creatures giggled with glee.

"But we love making a mess!" said the bat. "It's so much fun!" He turned the table over, tipping cakes everywhere.

The toad jumped into the splatters of icing with a chuckle, while the rat scuttled

over all the pretty tablecloths, leaving sticky pawprints everywhere. The crow hopped around excitedly as it helped the bat gather up more cakes to throw.

"Where did they come from?" asked Jess, ducking under a flying jam sponge cake.

"Probably the Witchy Waste," Goldie said grimly. "It's a gloomy place, near Grizelda's tower. It was once a beautiful water garden, with ponds, waterlilies, and willow trees. Then the naughty Witchy Waste creatures turned it into a big mess. It looks like a landfill now."

"That was horrible of them," said Lily.

"They're not really horrible," Goldie explained. "They like it that way—they just love messes!"

"Look!" Jess pointed to something floating through the trees toward them. It was a yellow-green orb. She knew exactly what that meant. "Grizelda's coming!"

They backed away as the orb exploded into smelly sparks.

The sparks cleared, revealing a tall, bony witch. Her green hair whipped around her head like squabbling snakes. She was wearing a purple tunic over tight

black pants that were tucked into boots
with skinny high heels.

"So you interfering girls are back," she
sneered. "But you won't win this time!
I have a new plan to take over Friendship
Forest! Ha!"

She beckoned to the messy creatures
from the Witchy Waste.

"These are my new helpers," she said.
"Don't meddle with them if you know
what's good for you."

The bat flapped onto her shoulder.

"This is Peep," said Grizelda, "and here
comes Masha."

 30

Masha the rat was wearing a crumpled straw hat with a droopy flower stuck into the band. She coiled her tail around the witch's leg, grinning.

"Snippit!" Grizelda called.

The scruffy crow, whose waistcoat had a button missing, flew to her other shoulder.

Grizelda nodded at the slimy toad, who straightened her necklace and waddled over. "I'm Hopper," she croaked.

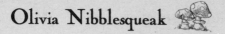

Grizelda laughed. "You girls won't be able to stop my new helpers. They're going to make the forest so messy that all the animals will have to leave. Then Friendship Forest will be mine!"

She raised her hands. Purple sparks shot from her fingers and crackled around each Witchy Waste creature.

Then, with a final cackle, Grizelda snapped her fingers and disappeared in a burst of smelly yellow sparks.

"Thank goodness she's gone," said Jess.

"What were those purple sparks?"

wondered Lily. "Do you think they're one of Grizelda's nasty spells?"

Goldie nodded. Her tail was twitching anxiously.

"Sparks made by Grizelda are sure to do something horrible," Jess sighed. "We'd better watch out!"

Now that Grizelda was gone, the animals began to come out from the bakery. Olivia was shaking icing from her rose crown.

"Squeeeaak!" Peep the bat flew straight toward her. He flapped his wings over

the little hamster, and the girls gasped
as the purple sparks reappeared and
crackled all around her.

"Heeheehee," giggled Peep the bat.
"This will be fun!"

Jess looked at Lily in alarm. "Oh no!
That bat did something to Olivia!" she
said. "But what?"

CHAPTER FOUR

Peep in the Night

Peep gave a high, squeaky giggle and turned to the Witchy Waste creatures. "Heeheehee, let's start messing up the forest, just like Grizelda said we should!"

The four messy animals disappeared into the trees.

Everyone gathered around Olivia. Her

little ears
were shaking
and her eyes
were wide and
scared.

"What were
those sparks?"
she asked in a
trembling voice.

Goldie hugged her. "We don't know,"
she said gently. "But everything will be
okay, we promise."

"I'm afraid the competition is
canceled," Mrs. Nibblesqueak announced.

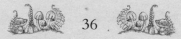

All the little animals looked sad, but everyone joined together to clean up the mess of cakes and splattered icing. Jess and Lily were so busy that they didn't realize how late it was until Goldie said, "It'll be dark soon. You should go home."

The girls glanced at each other.

How can we leave when Grizelda is threatening to ruin the forest again? Jess thought worriedly.

"We'd like to stay," said Lily, "so we can help if anything bad happens."

Jess nodded. "Back home, time stands

37

still while we're in Friendship Forest," she said, "so our parents won't be worried."

Goldie hugged them. "You're such good friends," she said. "We'll have a sleepover in my grotto—and then we'll all be ready to help Olivia, no matter what!"

"Squeeeeaaaak! Squeeeeaaaak!"

Lily woke with a start. "What's that noise?" she muttered, rubbing her eyes. She was snuggled in a nest of quilts and cushions on the floor of Goldie's grotto. It was lit by the soft glow of a night-light,

but she could see through the window in the door that it was dark outside.

Jess and Goldie had woken up, too, and were blinking sleepily.

"Squeeeeaaaak! Squeeeeaaaak!"

The noise came from just outside Goldie's grotto.

"What's happening?" Jess asked sleepily.

They went outside and found lots of animals in their pajamas, looking worried.

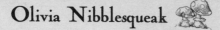

The whole Twinkletail mouse family was huddled together, wearing tiny pajamas. Lying all over the ground were torn

leaves and petals.

Mr. Muddlepup the dog came over. His nightcap drooped over one eye. "What's going on?" he yawned.

"It started outside our cottage," said Molly Twinkletail. "We followed the noise and it led us here to all these leaves. It's scary!"

Lily scooped her up. Molly was so small that Lily could hold her with just one hand. "Don't be afraid," she said. "We'll find out what's happening."

"Look!" said Jess. "There! Beneath that pine tree—two shadows!"

They crept closer.

"Squeeeeeeak!"

Just then, the shadows moved out into the moonlight.

"It's Peep . . . and Olivia!" cried Jess.

The bat ripped some leaves from a dandyrose bush and tossed them over his shoulder, while Olivia ripped the petals

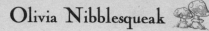

from a patch of buttercups. She threw
them up into the air.

Goldie gasped. "So they're the ones who
made this mess!"

"Squeeeeeeak!" went Peep.

"Squeeeeeeak!" went Olivia. Then Peep
flew to another bush and little Olivia
followed on the ground, flapping her paws.

"She's trying to fly like Peep!" cried Lily in dismay. "And she sounds like him, too!"

Peep reached out with his claws, picked up the little hamster, and flew onto a branch. Olivia flapped her paws, still trying to fly.

Molly covered her tiny ears as the horrible squeaking grew louder.

Lily cuddled her close and said to Jess and Goldie, "So that's what the purple spark spell does! Peep made Olivia act like a messy bat, just like him!"

Goldie gasped. "Oh, no!"

Jess stood beneath the tree. "Olivia!" she called. "Come down!"

"Won't!" squeaked Olivia.

Peep giggled. "This is fun!" he squeaked. "Soon Olivia will really turn into a bat, and then she'll be able to make another animal change, too. Then all the Friendship Forest animals will be messy and fun like me and my friends!"

The girls were horrified. "Imagine," said Jess, "a forest full of messy creatures."

Goldie nodded gloomily. "The whole forest will end up like the Witchy Waste," she said miserably.

 44

"And Grizelda will have Friendship Forest all for herself," Lily finished.

Just then, the rest of the Nibblesqueak family arrived, looking upset. "Where's our Olivia?" cried Mrs. Nibblesqueak. "Is—" She stopped and gasped when she saw her daughter flapping in the tree like a bat.

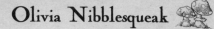

Jess put her arm around the shocked hamster comfortingly. "Don't worry," she said, patting her gently. "I promise we'll find a way to change Olivia back to her normal self."

She glanced anxiously at Lily, wondering how they could keep that promise.

But Lily had been thinking. "If we find out more about Peep's purple spark spell," she said, "we might find a way to undo it. Let's visit Mrs. Taptree!"

CHAPTER FIVE

Mrs. Taptree's Library

As the sun rose, Jess, Lily, and Goldie all headed for Mrs. Taptree's home.

"Here we are," said Goldie, stopping by a door in the broad trunk of a chestnut tree. As she knocked, the door flew open and a woodpecker popped out.

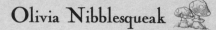

"Goodness, Goldie," she said, "you've brought Jess and Lily back to my library!"

"Hello, Mrs. Taptree," said the girls.

"Come in," said the woodpecker. "Quick! Quick!"

Jess and Lily had visited Mrs. Taptree's library before, but they still couldn't believe how much bigger it was on the inside than it looked on the outside!

Jess peered around for Mrs. Taptree's chicks. "Where are Dig and Tipper?"

The woodpecker pulled back a curtain of ivy leaves. There were her two chicks, fast asleep!

"They're tired out," said Mrs. Taptree. "That dreadful squeaking kept them up all night. Did you hear it?"

"That's why we're here," said Lily. She explained what had happened to Olivia. "We'd like to search your books for a way to break Peep's spell," she finished.

"Of course!" said Mrs. Taptree.

Jess went to the corner where three

 49

magical ladders stood and climbed on the
first one. "Hamsters!" she said.

Jess felt a thrill of excitement as her
ladder magically moved on its own,
sliding sideways into the "animal" section.
On the shelves, she spotted several books
all about hamsters.

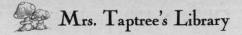

Goldie told her ladder, "Witches!"

Lily stood on the third one and said, "Bats!"

But as their ladders slid along, a loud "squeeeaaak!" came from above. It was Peep and Olivia, sitting up on a shelf!

"They must have snuck in after us!" cried Lily.

Peep flung a book to the ground. "Squeeeaaak!" he said happily.

"Please don't do that!" Mrs. Taptree begged, flapping her wings anxiously.

Olivia threw a book, too. "Making a

mess is fun!" she giggled, and pushed a whole row of books to the ground.

Mrs. Taptree grabbed a broom and took off, chasing Peep around the library. "Get out!" she squawked. "Leave my books alone! Quick! Quick!"

At last, Peep picked up Olivia and flapped out through the doorway. Jess, Lily, and Goldie started searching again.

"There's nothing about a bat spell," sighed Goldie.

52

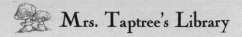

"Wait!" Lily said, reaching for the last book on the shelf. "I've found it!" she cried. "Purple spark transforming spell!"

She jumped off the ladder and flicked to the right page.

"And here's how to undo it! *A spell to turn you back to your normal self.*" She read it out loud:

"You want to be yourself again?
Then here's what you must do.
Gather up those favorite things
That mean the most to you.
What do you like to do the most?

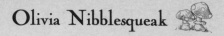

What food do you love the best?

And what is your biggest secret?

Now here's a little test.

Put them in your favorite place,

The place you love to be.

If someone names those things aloud,

Yourself once more you'll be."

"Hooray!" said Jess. She hugged Lily. "You've found the way to break the spell!"

She copied the spell into the little sketchbook she always kept in her pocket. "Now let's stop Grizelda's plan!"

CHAPTER SIX

Olivia's Favorites

When the three friends got back to the bakery, the Nibblesqueaks came scurrying outside to meet them.

"Have you seen Olivia?" asked Jenny Nibblesqueak.

Lily nodded. "Don't worry, she seems

fine. And we know how to help her!" She explained about the spell.

When she'd finished, Jess asked, "So what are Olivia's favorite things?"

Mr. Nibblesqueak said, "Her favorite hobby is easy. It's drawing!" He turned to Penny Nibblesqueak. "Could you fetch Olivia's art things?"

The young hamster scampered indoors and returned moments later with a sketchbook. She gave it to Jess, who flicked through it. It was just like the notebook she always kept in her pocket and was filled with colorful pictures.

"And what's Olivia's favorite food?"
Lily asked next.

"Pink cherries!" chorused the entire
family.

"She loves decorating cakes with them,"
said Mrs. Nibblesqueak, "but we don't
have any at the moment."

"We'll find some," said Goldie. "Now,
we need to discover Olivia's biggest secret.
But as it's a secret, I guess you probably
don't know what it is."

The hamsters shook their fluffy heads.

"Never mind," said Goldie. "We'll find out somehow. We know her favorite hobby and we have her sketchbook, so let's get some pink cherries."

"Off to the Treasure Tree!" said Jess, smiling at the thought of the huge tree that grew enough delicious fruit and nuts to feed everybody in the forest.

But Goldie shook her head. "Cherries don't grow on the Treasure Tree," she explained. "They grow in Cherry Tree Corner."

They said good-bye to the

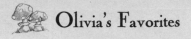

Nibblesqueaks, and Goldie led the girls through the forest to a huge sunny clearing filled with neat rows of cherry trees. Some were covered with clouds of pale pink blossoms, filling the air with their sweet scent. Others were drooping with bunches of fat, ripe cherries.

"It's so pretty," said Lily, breathing in the blossoms' scent.

"But there aren't any pink cherries!"
Jess cried. "They're all red."

"All of these cherries are magic,"
Goldie explained, "so maybe they're
called 'pink cherries' because of what
happens when you eat them." She looked
around, puzzled. "Each tree usually has a
label made of bark stuck into the ground
beside it—but they're all gone."

Just then, there was a loud squeak from
the far side of the orchard.

"Look!" cried Lily. "The creatures from
the Witchy Waste!"

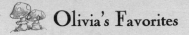

"And that's where the labels went," said Jess with a groan.

Beside Peep and the others was a pile of labels. Snippit the crow ripped one up with his beak and threw the pieces at Hopper the toad and Masha the rat, who shrieked with delight. Olivia giggled and flapped her paws around, squeaking like a naughty bat.

 61

Hopper spotted
the girls and Goldie. "There they are!"
she croaked. The four Witchy Waste
creatures and Olivia each grabbed some
cherries and flung them at Goldie and
the girls.

"Hey!" yelled Jess, as a cherry bounced
off her head.

"Oh, no!" Lily cried, as a cherry
splatted on her cheek.

"Hee!" laughed the rat. "You're messy!"

Jess ducked as more fruit flew past, then

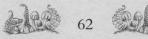

whispered
to the others,
"Keep them busy
while I ask Olivia
about pink cherries."

Lily grabbed a big handful of
cherries and tossed them at the Witchy
Waste creatures. "Catch!" she yelled.

As they yelled happily, throwing
more cherries back, Jess ducked down
and ran to the trees at the edge of the
clearing.

"Olivia!" Jess called. "Which tree do
pink cherries grow on?"

"Don't know," Olivia giggled. "Bats don't like cherries."

Jess groaned. *She really thinks she's a bat,* she thought.

She dodged the fruit and ran back to the others. They'd hidden behind a tree trunk, leaving the Witchy Waste creatures happily cherry-fighting among themselves. Splattered cherries lay everywhere.

"Now what?" Lily asked.

"I'll eat some," Jess said, "and see if we can tell which are pink ones."

She popped a cherry in her mouth.

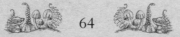

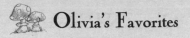

"Delicious!" she said. "And guess what? These cherries don't have stones. That's—" She stopped.

Goldie and Lily were almost helpless with laughter.

"What's funny?" Jess demanded.

"Your nose," Lily gasped. "It's covered with blue spots!"

"That must be the blue-spot cherry tree," Goldie said, giggling. "At least we know it's not those ones. Let's try another."

Lily popped a cherry in her mouth. Soon it was Jess's turn to laugh as Lily's cherry turned her cheeks bright green!

The first one Goldie tried made her whiskers curl, and Jess's next one gave her pointy ears!

When Lily ate a particularly large cherry, she noticed Jess and Goldie grinning.

"What?" she asked.

"You've found Olivia's favorite food," said Jess with a laugh, "and now we know what it does. Lily, your hair has turned pink!"

CHAPTER SEVEN

Bluebell Brook

Jess's cheeks and ears returned to normal.
Lily's nose and hair took a little longer,
and Goldie gave a sigh of relief when her
whiskers straightened out.

Lily put some pink cherries in her
pocket. "We know Olivia's favorite
hobby and her favorite food," she said,

"but we still haven't discovered her biggest secret . . ."

Jess thought for a moment. "Maybe Percy Littlepaw the vole would know," she said. "He's her best friend."

"Of course!" said Goldie. "Let's ask him—he lives next door to the bakery."

They hurried back and went straight to the Littlepaws' burrow in a grassy bank covered with climbing dandyroses.

Jess bent down to knock at the blue front door.

Percy opened it. "Have you found Olivia?" he asked anxiously.

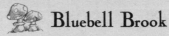

"No, we haven't," said Lily. Percy's whiskers drooped sadly. "You're Olivia's best friend," Jess said. "We need your help."

"Do you know what Olivia's secret is?" Lily asked.

"That's easy!" cried the little vole. "It's—" He stopped. "Oh! But it's not nice to tell someone's secret," he said.

Lily stroked his other paw. "Percy, it's okay to tell someone's secret if they're in trouble. We really need to know so we can save Olivia from Grizelda's magic."

Percy nodded. "All right," he said. "Her secret is her baby hamster doll, Nutmeg. Olivia thinks she's too old for Nutmeg now, so she plays with her in secret."

Goldie and the girls were delighted.

"Thanks, Percy!" said Lily. She blew him a kiss.

They hurried next door to the bakery. Mrs. Nibblesqueak rushed to answer their knock.

"We just need one more thing to save Olivia," Goldie explained. "It's Nutmeg!"

 70

But Mrs. Nibblesqueak wrung her paws with worry. "Oh dear," she said, "I haven't seen Olivia play with Nutmeg for months. I wonder where she is?"

Penny appeared in the doorway, too. "I'll search Olivia's room!" she said. But when she came back, she was shaking her head.

"I can't find Nutmeg anywhere," she said sadly. "Now what?" said Jess.

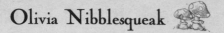

Mrs. Nibblesqueak's eyes filled with tears. "Will Olivia turn into a messy bat?" she asked with a sob.

Lily hugged her. "We're not going to let that happen," she promised. "We won't give up."

Mr. Nibblesqueak passed around cups of raspberry soda, and Goldie and the girls sat down to think about what to do next.

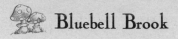

As she sipped her drink, Jess flicked through Olivia's sketchbook. "Here's a picture of you, Mrs. Nibblesqueak," she said. "And here's the Toadstool Café." She turned the page and found a drawing of a stream with bluebells growing along its banks. In tiny, hamster-size handwriting, Olivia had written *Bluebell Brook*.

Jess examined it closely, then gave a cry.

"That's lovely," Lily said.

"But look!" said Jess. "In the picture, something's tucked among the bluebells."

"It's a tiny hamster!" said Lily.

"Exactly," said Jess. "But maybe it's

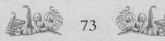

not a real hamster. Maybe it's Nutmeg
the hamster doll! If Olivia doesn't want
anyone to see her playing with it, maybe
she keeps it there—Bluebell Brook!" She
kept flipping through the sketchbook, and
they saw that Olivia had filled lots of other
pages with drawings of Bluebell Brook.

Lily was thrilled. "It must be her
favorite place!" She turned to Goldie and
the Nibblesqueaks. "Where is Bluebell
Brook?"

The Nibblesqueaks shook their heads.

"We don't know," said Olivia's dad, his
whiskers quivering with worry.

"There are lots of streams in the forest," said Goldie. "I've never heard of Bluebell Brook, but it's okay—I know someone who might have seen it. Captain Ace!"

A little later, Lily, Jess, and Goldie gazed down on the forest treetops. They were riding in a basket beneath a brightly colored patchwork hot air balloon!

Captain Ace flew alongside, towing the balloon with a rope in his beak. Whenever he squawked, "pull," Goldie tugged another rope that hung down inside the balloon.

Whoosh!

A stream of bubbles shot up into the hot air balloon, keeping it floating high up in the sky.

"Watch out for bluebells growing beside a brook," said Jess.

As they drifted along, Lily noticed a dark, forbidding building

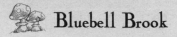

in the distance. "There's Grizelda's tower," she said, shivering.

"And see that gray area next to it?" said Goldie. "That's the Witchy Waste."

Now Jess shivered. "I'm glad we're not going there."

A few minutes later, Lily spotted a ribbon of sparkling water flowing lazily through a field of buttercups. All along its banks were drifts of blue flowers.

"Bluebell Brook!" she cried, pointing. "It must be!"

"Take us down, please, Captain Ace," Jess asked.

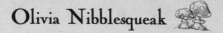

The balloon flew lower and lower, landing with a gentle bump among the pretty yellow buttercups.

"It looks just like Olivia's pictures!" Lily exclaimed.

The girls and Goldie climbed out and called, "Thanks, Captain!"

"Good luck!" he replied, and took off again.

The three friends headed toward the brook, where

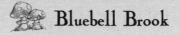

the water bubbled and gurgled over
moss-covered stones.

Goldie's ears pricked up. "Listen!"

They heard shrill squeaking.

"It's Peep and Olivia!" she said.
"They're coming this way."

They all crouched down, peering
between the bluebells.

They could hear Olivia giggling. "I
can't wait to make all these flowers messy,
too," she said. "Making a mess is so much
fun! I want to keep being messy forever
and ever!"

Peep flapped around her happily. "Not long to wait, Olivia," he said. "Grizelda said that it takes a day for the magic to work, so you'll turn into a bat really soon! Then we can be the messiest friends in the forest!"

Olivia gave a delighted squeak. "Hooray!" she cheered.

The girls and Goldie turned to each other in horror. "If our spell doesn't work," whispered Jess, "then Olivia really will turn into a bat—and there'll be nothing we can do to save her!"

CHAPTER EIGHT

Cakes for All!

Jess, Lily, and Goldie watched in horror as Olivia and Peep tore up the bluebells by Bluebell Brook. "Lovely mess!" squeaked Olivia, tossing the flowers into the bubbling water. Peep giggled and splashed the water with his wings.

Lily spotted a tiny figure among the

bluebells. "There's Nutmeg, Olivia's
toy hamster!" she whispered. "The spell
says that we need to gather all Olivia's
favorite things together. Come on!"

They wriggled on their stomachs
through the bluebells until they reached
Nutmeg.

Jess put the sketchbook beside the doll,
and Lily added the pink cherries. Then
Jess opened her notebook and read the
end of the spell:

"Put them in your favorite place,
The place you love to be.

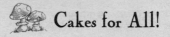

If someone names those things aloud,

Yourself once more you'll be."

"Look out," Lily whispered. "They're almost here!"

As Peep and Olivia came toward them, Goldie and the girls stood up.

"Olivia," Goldie said gently. "Look! All your favorite things, here in your favorite place."

The hamster came closer, flapping her paws, and sniffed the cherries and the sketchbook. Her whiskers quivered. When she saw Nutmeg, she gave a faint squeak.

"Now!" cried Lily.

"Olivia's favorite hobby . . ." Jess chanted, "is drawing!"

"Olivia's favorite food . . ." added Goldie, ". . . is pink cherries!"

"Olivia's biggest secret . . ." Lily shouted, ". . . is Nutmeg!"

They joined hands and said together: "Olivia's favorite place—Bluebell Brook!"

Instantly, purple sparks flew from Olivia out into the air. Her paws stopped flapping and she stopped squeaking.

Jess and Lily jumped for joy. "Hooray!"

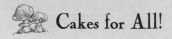

"We did it!" said Goldie.

The little hamster looked confused.

Lily scooped her up and cuddled her.

"Everything's all right," she said softly, dropping a kiss on her golden-brown head.

Olivia clung to her. "I'm glad to see you," she said. "Something really funny happened to me."

"You've been under a spell," Jess explained, "but we've broken the magic."

"Thank you," said Olivia. "I'm glad I feel like me again!"

"Oh, no!" cried Peep. He flapped around them, squeaking angrily. "Now we can't make a mess together! Olivia won't be any fun to play with anymore!"

"You shouldn't be making a mess in the forest, Peep!" said Goldie sternly. "The animals don't like their home being spoiled!"

But Peep didn't seem to have heard her. "I'm going to find my friends," he said to himself, "then we can make some lovely new messes!" And he flapped away.

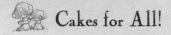

Jess sighed. "Oh, dear! I hope he doesn't cause too much trouble." Then she spotted something floating toward them. It was the familiar yellow-green orb.

"Look out!" she cried. "Grizelda!"

Olivia put her paws over her eyes as the orb exploded in a shower of smelly sparks. The witch's green hair was so wild it

was tying itself in knots. "You might have won this time," she snarled, "but I've got three more Witchy Waste creatures. This isn't over! Friendship Forest will be mine!"

She snapped her fingers and disappeared in a shower of stinky sparks.

Olivia uncovered her eyes. "Thank goodness she's gone," she said. "Now let's go home!"

Goldie, Jess, and Lily stood outside the Nibblesqueak Bakery, surrounded by their friends. The cake-decorating competition had started again, and everyone was having fun with Eezy-Skweezy Bags and Nibblesqueaks' Famous Nectar Icing.

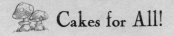

Olivia's parents and sisters couldn't stop hugging her.

"Thank you, Lily and Jess," said Olivia's mom. "And thank you, Goldie. You've saved Olivia from becoming a messy bat forever. You're all so clever."

"And brave," said Olivia. "That witch is really scary!"

"I wonder," said Mr. Nibblesqueak, "if Jess and Lily would like to judge the cake-decorating competition?"

The girls were thrilled. They sat on the soft green grass and the little animals all brought their cakes up to be judged. Lucy

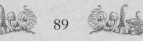

Longwhiskers had iced carrots around the edge of her cake, and Molly Twinkletail's was covered in tiny pink and blue flowers.

"They're all so beautiful," Lily said to Jess as she admired Sophie Flufftail's sunflower design. "But I know which cake should win."

"Me, too!" said Jess. She whispered in Lily's ear, and Lily smiled and nodded.

Then the two girls announced together, "The winner is . . . Percy Littlepaw!"

Percy gasped with delight as Lily put a red rosette on his cake. It was decorated

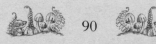

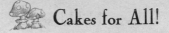

like a patchwork hot air balloon with a little icing Captain Ace flying beside it.

Everyone cheered! Percy got a special hug from Olivia, who presented the prize—an enormous basket of hazelnut and raspberry muffins.

"Wow!" he said.

"And I've iced cherry cupcakes for everyone!" said Olivia. She scurried around with a tray laden with pink cupcakes, each with a cherry on top.

The girls and Goldie glanced at each other as everyone ate the cakes. They guessed what was about to happen.

Lucy Longwhiskers burst out laughing. "Molly, your fur's bright pink!"

The little mouse giggled. "So are your ears, Lucy!"

"And my feathers!" said Ellie Featherbill the duckling.

Everyone had turned pink!

Jess, Lily, and Goldie ate their cakes, and, in moments, the girls' hair was bright pink, and Goldie's fur was as pink as all the other animals'.

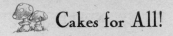

Olivia laughed. "Pink cherries are definitely my favorite!"

When the cupcakes were gone, everyone headed home, clutching party bags full of coconut custard éclairs.

It was time for the girls to leave, too.

"Good-bye, Olivia," they said.

The hamster held Nutmeg's paw and

made her wave good-bye. "I don't mind anyone knowing I play with her now," she said. "If it wasn't for Nutmeg, I'd have turned into a bat!"

After lots of hugs and waves, Jess and Lily followed Goldie back to the Friendship Tree.

The cat touched a paw to the trunk, and the door opened, revealing a magical golden glow.

"Thank you for stopping Grizelda's nasty plans again," Goldie said, hugging them good-bye.

"She has three more Witchy Waste

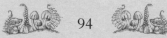

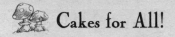

creatures to make the forest messy," said
Jess. "When they do, we'll help."

Lily nodded. "We'll never let Friendship
Forest down."

"I know," said Goldie. "We're so lucky
to have you as our special friends." She
hugged them. "Good-bye. See you soon!"

The girls entered the golden light.
They felt the tingle that meant they were
returning to their normal size. When the
light faded, they found themselves back in
Brightley Meadow.

"What an adventure!" Lily said.

"I can't wait for our next one!" said Jess.

They raced back to Helping Paw,
where they found the animals nibbling
the special treats they had baked.

"They're enjoying them," said Lily.
"Let's make some more."

"Maybe we could decorate them!"
Jess laughed. "If only we had some of
Nibblesqueaks' Famous Nectar Icing!"

"And Olivia's pink cherries!" said Lily,
and the girls laughed as they ran into
the barn.

The End

Lily and Jess are excited to visit Friendship Forest for Blossom Day, but Grizelda has a terrible trick in store! When Grizelda casts a spell on Evie Scruffypup to make all Evie's fun surprises mischievious ones, can the girls undo the spell before Blossom Day is ruined?

Find out in their next adventure,

Evie Scruffypup's Big Surprise

Turn the page for a sneak peek ...

Evie and Hattie climbed into the tree house. Then they vanished from sight!

"Where are you?" Lily called up.

"Surprise!" Evie giggled, popping up at a third floor window.

Laughing, the girls and Goldie followed them inside. Evie gave a *yip* of excitement, and held up a small packet made of leaves tied with grass strands. "Surprise!" she called. "Blossom drops!"

She handed the parcel to Lily, who opened it. Inside were lots of oval, honeysuckle-scented treats.

"Mmm!" Lily said as she ate one.

"It's gooey in the middle! That was a surprise."

Evie giggled and Hattie pulled her into a hug. "Evie loves surprises!" Hattie said, ruffling her little sister's fluffy fur.

They all jumped as there was a terrified squeal.

"Eeeeeeeek!"

It came from the Scruffypups' den.

Read

Evie Scruffypup's Big Surprise

to find out what happens next!

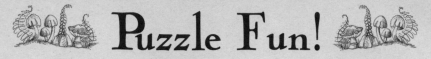

Puzzle Fun!

Olivia Nibblesqueak has jumbled up all these words into a mess! Can you work out what they should say?

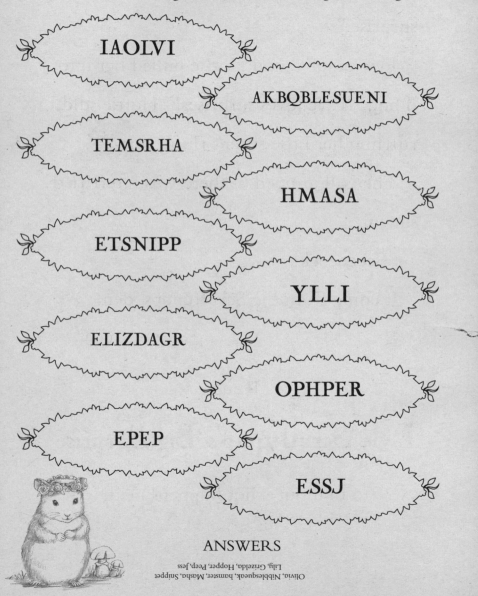

IAOLVI

AKBQBLESUENI

TEMSRHA

HMASA

ETSNIPP

YLLI

ELIZDAGR

OPHPER

EPEP

ESSJ

ANSWERS

Lily and Jess's Animal Facts

Lily and Jess love lots of different animals—
both in Friendship Forest
and in the real world.

Here are their top facts about

HAMSTERS

like Olivia Nibblesqueak.

- Hamsters are nocturnal animals, which means they sleep during the day and are awake at night.

- Hamsters can live up to three years.

- Male hamsters are called boars, females are called sows, and baby hamsters are called pups.

- Golden hamsters have four toes on their front paws, but they have five on their back ones!

RAINBOW magic ™

Which Magical Fairies Have You Met?

- ❏ The Rainbow Fairies
- ❏ The Weather Fairies
- ❏ The Jewel Fairies
- ❏ The Pet Fairies
- ❏ The Dance Fairies
- ❏ The Music Fairies
- ❏ The Sports Fairies
- ❏ The Party Fairies
- ❏ The Ocean Fairies
- ❏ The Night Fairies
- ❏ The Magical Animal Fairies
- ❏ The Princess Fairies
- ❏ The Superstar Fairies
- ❏ The Fashion Fairies
- ❏ The Sugar & Spice Fairies
- ❏ The Earth Fairies
- ❏ The Magical Crafts Fairies
- ❏ The Baby Animal Rescue Fairies
- ❏ The Fairy Tale Fairies

📖 SCHOLASTIC

Find all of your favorite fairy friends at
scholastic.com/rainbowmagic

HIT entertainment

RMFAIRY13